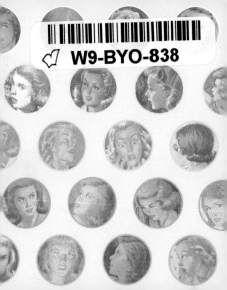

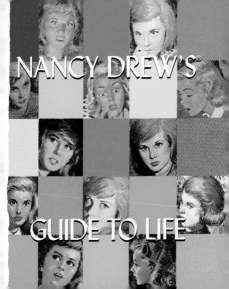

NANCY DREW'S®

GUIDE TO LIFE

A Running Press® Miniature Edition™
© 2001 by Running Press
All rights reserved under the Pan-American
and International Copyright Conventions
Printed in China

*Nancy Drew® is a registered trademark of Simon &
Schuster, Inc. This edition is published by arrangement
with Simon & Schuster, Inc.*

Library of Congress
Cataloging-in-Publication Number 2001087098

ISBN-13: 978-0-7624-1085-9
ISBN-10: 0-7624-1085-X

This book may be ordered by mail from the publisher.
Please include $1.00 for postage and handling.
But try your bookstore first!

Running Press Book Publishers
2300 Chestnut Street
Philadelphia, PA 19103-4371

Visit us on the web!
www.runningpress.com

Nancy Drew's®
Guide to Life

by Jennifer Worick

Running Press
Philadelphia · London

Contents

Introduction 6

1 Survival Strategies 10

2 Dating: A Primer 26

3 Sleuthing 101 40

4  The Delicate Art of Etiquette . . 58

5 Wilderness Tips 80

6 On Being a Lady 96

7 Powers of Observation 110

8 Accoutrements 127

Role model? Definitely.
Genius? Oh, yeah.
Goddess? Probably.

It continues to be Nancy Drew who delights and inspires young girls everywhere. From her home base in River Heights, USA, Nancy has taken us on mysterious adventures around the world. We've traveled vicariously to Turkey in *The Mysterious Mannequin.* We enjoyed a tour of Scotland in *The Clue of the Whistling Bagpipes*. Through all this, we've joined Nancy, Bess, George, Ned, Hannah, and Mr. Carson Drew, Esq., in their investigations into all things untoward.

While we have grown from 12-year-old sleuths into adults, Nancy has remained a spunky, titian-haired 18 year old.

And don't forget she's a genius.

Nancy Drew's® Guide to Life is a loving tribute to the young gumshoe and the wisdom she imparted to us. We would never have thought of reviving someone with our purse-sized vial of Chanel No. 19. And who would have suspected that it isn't wise to buy stock from a door-to-door saleswoman? Nancy, that's who.

You couldn't have known

it then, but all those hours spent reading about Nancy's adventures served you well in life. *Nancy Drew's® Guide to Life* is filled with humorous and practical wisdom from our favorite sleuth from River Heights.

For every woman who remembers wishing she could tail a suspicious truck in Nancy's smart blue roadster with the rest of the gang, this book is for you.

Chapter 1
Survival
Strategies

If the ceiling collapses,
breathe through a handkerchief
to avoid inhaling dust.
—*The Hidden Staircase*

Moxie and a good
sense of balance
are essential when
crawling on a roof.
—*The Hidden Staircase*

When your ride is mired in mud, placing heavy burlap in front of the rear wheels and rocking the car back and forth can get you back on the road.

—*The Secret of Red Gate Farm*

If you lack backup when you happen upon crooks caught in the act, disguise your voice and pretend to be the police. If that fails to produce the desired result, throw a stone through a window to feign a gunshot.
—*The Sign of the Twisted Candles*

When bound and gagged, you can still tap out HELP in Morse code to attract attention.
—*The Clue of the Tapping Heels*

Don't hide in a phone booth. Someone could turn the tables on you and trap you in it by wedging a piece of wood under the door.
—*The Clue in the Jewel Box*

It's prudent when traveling in a group to take more than one vehicle. If one car slides into a ditch, the other can pull the disabled car out.

—*Mystery at the Ski Jump*

In the event of a carjacking, try to steer the vehicle toward the house of an off-duty state trooper or police officer. Of course, it helps to know where the aforementioned officer of the law resides.

—*The Scarlet Slipper Mystery*

Don't overlook the tried and true. If caught in a housefire, don't hesitate to tie sheets and blankets together to swing to safety.

—*The Scarlet Slipper Mystery*

Don't let strangers lock up your house after you.

—*The Witch Tree Symbol*

Loophole in moral code: It's okay to steal a car if it belongs to your kidnappers.
—*The Whispering Statue*

If your chum (instead of you) gets a call that your parent is hovering at death's door, it may be a hoax.
—*The Witch Tree Symbol*

Bouncing a car makes it easier to move if it's in a tight spot.
—*The Haunted Showboat*

Flowers sent by secret admirers might be coated with poison.
—*The Secret of the Golden Pavilion*

Cover your face immediately when confronted with an explosion. Obviously, it is good to avoid explosions in general.
—*The Mystery of the Fire Dragon*

If someone other than a legitimate cop stops you in your car and asks you to roll down the window, lay on the horn to attract attention.
—*The Clue of the Dancing Puppet*

If you hear the telltale sounds of a helicopter, step away from a blaze in the fireplace. The copter might send a downdraft into the chimney and shower sparks all over your sleek coif.

—*The Mystery of the 99 Steps*

Don't let a stranger's lame attempt to appear ill lull you into letting down your defenses if you are alone. Keep your car door locked!
—*The Mystery of the 99 Steps*

If acid finds its way onto your skin, dip the burning area in mineral oil for quick relief.
—*The Spider Sapphire Mystery*

When pinned down by a large canine, instruct friends, family, even random passersby to direct a hose on the beast.
—*The Mysterious Mannequin*

Stink bombs are effective intimidation tactics.
—*The Double Jinx Mystery*

Always lock your car doors. Even if there's nothing in the vehicle to take, a devilish person can always put something harmful *into* the car.
—*The Secret of the Forgotten City*

Chapter 2
Dating:
A Primer

Make your date work for you—send him on B-level errands you can't seem to fit into your busy schedule.
—*The Clue in the Diary*

If a guy keeps driving you around on his motorcycle so you can run pointless errands, he probably likes you.
—*The Message in the Hollow Oak*

Clumsy, fat men who are looking at middle age through a rear-view mirror should not attempt to keep pace with lithe young women.
—*The Whispering Statue*

A young lady with some judo skills can take care of unwanted advances in short order.
—*The Whispering Statue*

Make sure rendezvous notes were actually sent by the cutie you've had your eye on. Otherwise, you might find yourself treading water while your ship sails on without you.
—*Mystery of the Brass-Bound Trunk*

If a guy takes you on a roller coaster repeatedly, it might be because he likes it when you cling to him.
—*The Clue in the Jewel Box*

You can tell a lot about a man by his hands.
—*The Clue in the Jewel Box*

Boys like girls who doggedly pursue their goals (or prey, as the case may be).
—*The Secret of the Wooden Lady*

A forceful and skilled dance partner will make you forget everything on your mind.
—*The Clue of the Velvet Mask*

Keep your boyfriend guessing. Letting him know you're spending time with another man (even if you don't happen to mention he's a suspect or a key part of your case) can keep an admirer working hard to win your affections.
—*The Hidden Window Mystery*

If you want to move in on a promising young man, acting opposite him in a love scene doesn't always guarantee true romance will follow.
—*The Clue of the Dancing Puppet*

The best way to lose a boy is to chase after him.
—*The Clue of the Dancing Puppet*

If a guy's hunch results in a dead-end, don't flaunt your better judgment and intuition in front of him. Smirk secretly to yourself.
—*The Phantom of Pine Hill*

The perfect man? Tall, handsome, good company, and lots of fun but serious and practical when help is needed.
—*The Invisible Intruder*

Come up with a clever code with your beau in case one of you is ever kidnapped.
—*The Invisible Intruder*

Male fireflies turn their lights on and off in unison while the females flicker whenever they please. Perhaps there's a correlation to be made?
—*The Secret of Mirror Bay*

Don't force your date to go to a ballet or another activity that may not be to his liking if he was knocked unconscious earlier in the day.
—*The Double Jinx Mystery*

When choosing between two men, take into consideration the different paths your life would take should you go with either of them.
—*The Sky Phantom*

After receiving an electrical shock to the system, find as many men as possible to vigorously massage you.
—*Mystery of the Glowing Eye*

Chapter 3
Sleuthing
101

Never sleuth on an empty stomach.
—*The Hidden Staircase*

College archeological digs are perfect
covers for undercover sleuthing.
That is, if you can pass for a coed.
—*The Message in the Hollow Oak*

Making thugs turn on each other is
always a delicious thing to watch.
—*The Whispering Statue*

Don't release a runaway circus
animal without some identification
from the claimant.
—*The Mystery at the Moss-Covered Mansion*

If you suspect that an important message or map will be pilfered, make a copy and alter the facts to throw creeps off the trail. Or make a copy and send the original to a close friend for safekeeping.
—*The Quest of the Missing Map*

It doesn't hurt to question a person appearing sick. The illness might be a devious ruse to dupe you.
—*The Clue in the Jewel Box*

When trying to investigate a property that's off limits, consider putting your flying lessons to good use and fly over the area.
—*The Clue in the Crumbling Wall*

To protect and earmark footprints, ring them with stones.
—*The Clue of the Dancing Puppet*

When forging a letter to nab a perp, be sure to use grammar and spelling appropriate to the education level of the person you're impersonating.
—*The Ghost of Blackwood Hall*

When confused, sit back and try to arrange the facts into some kind of order.
—*The Ghost of Blackwood Hall*

Train your friends in the art of investigation. You could save their lives if they remember your teachings.
—*The Clue of the Black Keys*

When you want to know if and where a location exists in the state, simply call the state capitol.
—*Mystery at the Ski Jump*

Being able to throw your voice can get your unskilled assistants out of tight jams.
—*The Ringmaster's Secret*

Convertibles are swell but they sure do call attention to your comings and goings.
—*The Haunted Showboat*

Bluffing about questionable information can often lead to people revealing juicy secrets.
—*The Clue in the Old Stagecoach*

When checking out a suspect's lair, note that it is illegal to open any drawers or closets.
—*The Mystery of the Fire Dragon*

If you suspect a gang is using a password, you can try to gain access to the inner circle by mentioning the name of their current hangout.
—*The Clue of the Dancing Puppet*

When searching a house or apartment, don't forget to check the oven. It's a pretty roomy hiding space.
—*The Clue of the Dancing Puppet*

When investigating a building with a fellow sleuth, look ahead and to the right while your companion looks behind you and to the left. Clever!
—*The Moonstone Castle Mystery*

To stop crooks from making a clean getaway, drain the gas out of the tank, let the air out of the tires, and take the key if it's in the ignition.
—*The Spider Sapphire Mystery*

When trying to crack a numerical code, don't rule out latitude and longitude coordinates.
—*The Spider Sapphire Mystery*

When searching for important clues, anything labeled "Top Secret" might be a good place to start.
—*The Crooked Banister*

When examining mug shots, try to envision how a suspect in an old photograph may have aged, grown facial hair, lost or put on weight, and otherwise altered his or her appearance.
—*The Double Jinx Mystery*

A soft, kindly approach to questioning prisoners can make them squeal.
—*Mystery of Crocodile Island*

Spend time at the gym to build upper body strength. Detective work may require fending off a vicious hair pulling.
—*The Thirteenth Pearl*

Chapter 4
The Delicate Art of Etiquette

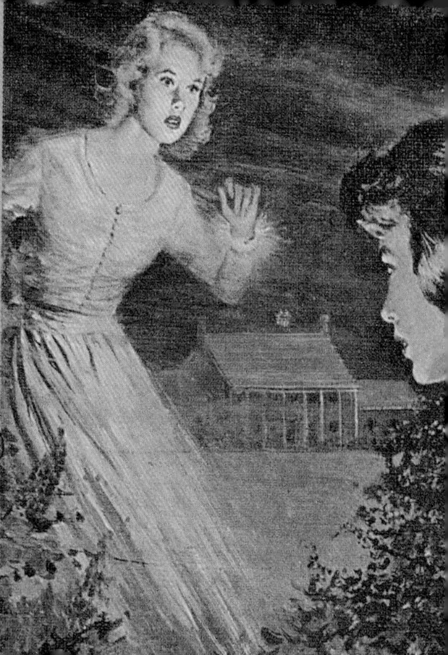

Don't let your troubles get in the way of enjoying a leisurely and delightful lunch.
—*The Secret of the Old Clock*

Any woman who asks to be introduced to your widowed father is bad news.
—*The Mystery of Lilac Inn*

Even with an active lifestyle, being prompt is important.
—*The Secret of Red Gate Farm*

Don't say "well" all the time.
It's far from well.

—*Nancy's Mysterious Letter*

It's good to toast space
exploration and fancy gadgets,
but it's more important to
raise a glass to the beauty
of soft candlelight.

—*The Sign of the Twisted Candles*

Do not press new acquaintances
to talk if they are visibly upset.

—*The Clue of the Broken Locket*

Don't proffer information
about valuable family
heirlooms to strangers.
—*The Clue of the Broken Locket*

Beware the stranger on
the plane who grills you
for personal information.
—*The Message in the Hollow Oak*

Call before driving a
considerable distance
to talk with someone.
—*The Mystery at the
Moss-Covered Mansion*

Offer an ill-at-ease visitor coffee to give him time to compose himself.
—*The Secret in the Old Attic*

Dressing well will open any doors, even those connected to a top-secret factory.
—*The Secret in the Old Attic*

A sincere and straightforward demeanor will get most anyone to open up and volunteer information. It doesn't hurt to be an attractive young woman, either.
—*The Clue in the Old Album*

Learning a new craft will make you chatter on incessantly about the art form. Be careful not to bore your less artsy friends.
—*The Clue of the Leaning Chimney*

Humor the older generation and do a few activities once in a while that they'll enjoy.
—*The Clue of the Leaning Chimney*

A good hostess directs guests away from an elderly friend's favorite chair.
—*The Hidden Window Mystery*

No one is so jaded that they don't appreciate praise for mysteries solved or jobs well done, no matter how small.
—*The Hidden Window Mystery*

An air of superiority can
ruin a first impression.
—*The Haunted Showboat*

Never interrupt a
voodoo doctor.
—*The Haunted Showboat*

Aggressiveness will not
earn you an invitation to
sit at the popular table.
—*The Clue in the Old Stagecoach*

It's important to take time out to have fun with your friends, particularly if they spend considerable time doing your bidding.

—*The Clue in the Old Stagecoach*

Ply testy taxi drivers with compliments.

—*The Mystery of the Fire Dragon*

It's a bit gratuitous to quote passages from Shakespeare on a daily basis.

—*The Clue of the Dancing Puppet*

Never take sides when friends who are related to each other are in disagreement.
—*The Moonstone Castle Mystery*

Name-dropping your famous parent will spring you from the hoosegow pretty much all the time.
—*The Moonstone Castle Mystery*

Invite an unfairly accused suspect to assist you in a task to show you have complete confidence in him.
—*The Clue of the Whistling Bagpipes*

Don't let a friend strong-arm you into forgoing your agenda for her own pursuit of fun.
—*The Mystery of the 99 Steps*

Play up to your hosts by complimenting their children.
—*The Mystery of the 99 Steps*

It's okay to accept free trips from your friend's parents, but only if they are exceedingly rich.
—*The Clue in the Crossword Cipher*

To defuse a situation involving your friend and her two jealous suitors, try regaling the group with stories of *your* harrowing adventures.
—*The Sky Phantom*

If grilling a salesperson or shop owner for information, it's only proper to buy a few articles from the establishment.
—*The Strange Message in the Parchment*

To alleviate a guest's embarrassment over breaking or damaging an object, a good host or hostess will continue the conversation to divert attention from the incident.
—*The Thirteenth Pearl*

Chapter 5
Wilderness Tips

A bright overhead light will dull an owl's vision enough to remove it from indoors. Of course, thick gloves and quick reflexes help.
—*The Hidden Staircase*

The best way to clear one's mind is to commune with nature.
—*The Hidden Staircase*

If you see something resembling a shark in a river, don't fret. It's more likely to be a small submarine operated by thieves.
—*The Mystery of Lilac Inn*

When lost in the mountains, caves are excellent shelters.
—*The Secret at Shadow Ranch*

It's a good idea to arm yourself when in the wilderness because you might just have to kill a large lynx.
—*The Secret at Shadow Ranch*

When witnessing a massive fire, take careful note of shifts in the wind's direction.
—*The Clue in the Diary*

If you see a child bobbing directly in the path of a speedboat, grab the kid and dive down under the boat until you see it pass over you. Hope that the child can hold her breath.
—*Password to Larkspur Lane*

A loon's call can often be mistaken for a woman's scream.
—*The Clue of the Broken Locket*

Don't try to ford rocky streams in an old jalopy.
—*The Message in the Hollow Oak*

If you lose sight of a suspect amongst trees and foliage, try putting an ear to the ground to detect the footsteps.
—*The Clue in the Crumbling Wall*

When thrust into darkness, close your eyes for several seconds; it helps you to adjust to the darkness.
—*The Ghost of Blackwood Hall*

Snowmen on ski slopes make excellent hiding places.
—*Mystery at the Ski Jump*

A swamp might be stinky, but head for the areas rich in moss: the aforementioned flora actually purifies the air.
—*The Haunted Showboat*

Adventure can make you hungry! Pack a hearty snack.
—*The Moonstone Castle Mystery*

Simple screaming can scare off snakes.
—*Mystery of Crocodile Island*

Runaway horses can sense if you are kind and will slow down.
—*The Crooked Banister*

In the event of a scorpion sting: Tie a tourniquet near the puncture between the sting and the victim's heart. Put an ice pack over the sting or fill a bowl or bucket with half ice and half water and submerge the stung area.
—*The Secret of the Forgotten City*

To avoid being spotted from overhead by a snoop in an airplane, try curling up, putting your head inside your dark sweater, and blending into the landscape.
—*The Sky Phantom*

If a bleeding, screaming man runs from shore and starts swimming frantically toward your boat, you should probably help him out. He might be escaping from cruel employers.
—*Mystery of Crocodile Island*

Dive into any available water when attacked by a swarm of mosquitoes.
—*Mystery of Crocodile Island*

Gesticulate like crazy to stop an ornery ox.
—*The Clue in the Crossword Cipher*

Chapter 6
On Being
a Lady

A face distorted with anger will only accentuate a person's innate ugliness.
—*The Secret of the Old Clock*

When the lights suddenly go out, hold onto your diamonds for dear life.
—*The Mystery of Lilac Inn*

Use common sense in buying. If you have a clothing budget, make sure your pricier items are worth forfeiting lots of sensible basics.
—*Nancy's Mysterious Letter*

No complimentary makeup application ever looks good, especially when applied by a gypsy woman with an outdoor cart. Derivative lesson: The perfume she sells is probably watered down.
—*The Mystery of the Tolling Bell*

When shopping with your friends, take into consideration their personal tastes when they comment on the outfit you are trying on. If your friend calls a dress "fussy," it may be because she always wears casual togs. Consider the source and if possible, shop with a friend whose style you admire.
—*The Clue of the Black Keys*

Don't let your one-track mind interfere with your tennis game when playing doubles. You could let yourself and your partner down.
—*The Clue of the Black Keys*

Never lose your girlish glee when your dad buys you a ticket to Hong Kong.
—*The Mystery of the Fire Dragon*

Lipstick is not just for looking glamorous; it can be used to signal for help on windows or other surfaces.
—*The Mystery of the Fire Dragon*

Beware door-to-door saleswomen selling stock in fur companies (also beware door-to-door saleswomen selling stock in maverick cosmetic companies, as demonstrated in *The Mystery of the Tolling Bell*).
—*Mystery at the Ski Jump*

A mysterious expression will add a lovely sheen to your complexion.
—*The Clue of the Velvet Mask*

When you have big news to divulge at dinner, it's advisable to take great care in planning the menu.
—*The Clue of the Dancing Puppet*

Don't let fear mean more
to you than your friends.
—*The Clue of the Velvet Mask*

If you can at all prevent it,
do not chase after thieves when
you are clad only in a leotard.
It's unseemly.
—*The Scarlet Slipper Mystery*

Don't wear expensive jewelry
to the circus. A clown might
notice it and try to lift it.
—*The Ringmaster's Secret*

Determination and spunk can elicit admiration from many arenas, even from the criminal element.
—*The Phantom of Pine Hill*

You can never really be yourself and "let your hair down" if you're sporting a wig.
—*The Spider Sapphire Mystery*

Stick to simple fare and favorite recipes when unexpectedly cooking dinner for a group.
—*The Double Jinx Mystery*

Chapter 7
Powers of
Observation

If you spot a disdainful shopper damaging an item and then walking away, you may be able to snatch it up at a serious price reduction.
—*The Secret of the Old Clock*

If you see a downed pigeon, check to see if it's ferrying any messages. It might be a carrier pigeon.
—*Password to Larkspur Lane*

Strange mechanical noises can only mean one thing: a printing press is being used for nefarious purposes.
—*The Clue of the Broken Locket*

Young boys who stand tall and with dignity are certainly not the fruit of a cruel, dictatorial man's loins. It simply isn't in the genes.
—*The Mystery of the Ivory Charm*

Abandoned houses are not completely neglected if the electricity still flows.
—*The Mystery of the Ivory Charm*

Don't discount faint lines or indecipherable blotches on discarded pieces of paper. A magnifying glass might reveal them to be very small words.
—*Mystery of the Brass-Bound Trunk*

Any unusual mounds of dirt
could indicate recent digging.
—*The Mystery at the Moss-Covered Mansion*

If an heir to a fortune isn't even trying
to feign grief over a relative's death,
he or she just might be trying to steal
an inheritance.
—*The Mystery at the Moss-Covered Mansion*

Doodling as a child might be a sign of
artistic aptitude and a promising career.
—*The Quest of the Missing Map*

A strange tattoo might be a means
of identifying long-lost royalty.
—*The Clue in the Jewel Box*

Take careful note of distinct odors; they can prove to be valuable clues.
—*The Secret in the Old Attic*

Postmarks and return addresses are important clues!
—*The Clue of the Black Keys*

When cornered in a hotel room or ship's berth, look for a bell cord to signal for help.
—*The Secret of the Wooden Lady*

If you are interrogating a
suspected thief in his home
or trailer, note whether his
eyes dart to any possible
hiding place in the room.
—*The Ringmaster's Secret*

If someone pays for an
expensive item in cash,
the bills could well be
funny money.
—*The Witch Tree Symbol*

If tied up by a culprit, note
whether they used any fancy
nautical knots. It might be
a valuable clue.
—*The Clue in the Old Stagecoach*

Podunk towns just might surprise you with sophisticated night clubs, if you canvass the outskirts of town.
—*The Moonstone Castle Mystery*

College undergrads can discern harmless knockout drops from more dangerous poison. Isn't Ned dreamy?
—*The Moonstone Castle Mystery*

Bold, vertical handwriting usually belongs to a literary person, and jerky, slanted-to-the-right letters are a sign of nervousness.
—*The Clue of the Whistling Bagpipes*

While you can't tell from a footprint whether someone is a crook, you can estimate weight, height, and the speed at which the person was walking or running.
—*The Secret of Mirror Bay*

When the FBI shows up, make sure they are toting proper identification. Don't put it past shady characters to impersonate G-men.
—*Mystery of the Glowing Eye*

Law associates that are cooking snazzy French meals for your single lawyer dad might have designs on him.
—*Mystery of the Glowing Eye*

Clothing may provide a clue to someone's name; check for any special lettering or monograms.
—*The Strange Message in the Parchment*

When examining tire treads, note any unique markings or insignias from the tire manufacturer.
—*The Thirteenth Pearl*

Chapter 8
Accoutrements

Take matches from restaurants and hotel dining rooms. You just might need them to light a kerosene lamp!
—*The Bungalow Mystery*

Keep an extra flashlight in your glove compartment and take a course in auto mechanics. You never know when you'll need to repair a sabotaged convertible.
—*The Bungalow Mystery*

It's helpful to pack a spare set of diving gear because you never know when your equipment will be damaged by a rogue spear.
—*The Mystery of Lilac Inn*

In a pinch, a vial of perfume can sterilize scissors.
—*The Secret of Red Gate Farm*

If you are afraid of being followed when you leave your house, buy a new car and have it brought around to the back of the house for a sneaky escape.
—*Password to Larkspur Lane*

Keep a flashlight under your pillow. It sure comes in handy when awakened from a dead sleep by a wild animal.
—*The Message in the Hollow Oak*

Good-luck talismans can't hurt.
—*The Mystery of the Ivory Charm*

Spike heels come in handy when it is necessary to break glass.
—*Nancy's Mysterious Letter*

Tap dance lessons + Morse code = ingenious combination.
—*The Clue of the Tapping Heels*

Some schooling in antiques can help ferret valuable baubles out of an attic and assist a down-on-his-luck curmudgeon.
—*The Secret in the Old Attic*

Don't pass up a great deal on a used sailboat because of a sorry paint job. It could be a real gem.
—*The Clue in the Old Album*

A bottle of phosphorus and oil will produce an eerie green light for spectral shenanigans.
—*The Ghost of Blackwood Hall*

Tying burlap bags over
your shoes will help
obscure your footprint.
—*The Clue of the Leaning Chimney*

Keep your ice skates sharpened.
You just might be called upon
to impersonate a figure skater.
—*Mystery at the Ski Jump*

The key to trick horseback
riding is precise timing.
—*The Ringmaster's Secret*

ACCOUTREMENTS 138

Always carry your birth certificate with you; you never know when you will need it.
—*The Mystery of the Fire Dragon*

Owning your own key-making machine can be quite handy, and a compact one can be stored out of sight under the sink so as not to clash with your décor.
—*The Phantom of Pine Hill*

Since it is out of vogue to carry around smelling salts, you can try reviving someone with a small vial of perfume.
—*The Mystery of the 99 Steps*

Carrying paper and colored pencils can allow you to sketch rough portraits of missing persons and suspects.
—*The Mysterious Mannequin*

Use protective eyewear when chiseling stone.
—*The Secret of the Forgotten City*

Carry a police whistle to scare off creeps.
—*The Secret of the Forgotten City*

A fagot is a bundle of tightly woven twigs, like a basket. Just a good fact to know.
—*The Secret of the Forgotten City*

Nancy Drew®
Mystery Stories

The Secret of the Old Clock (#1)

The Hidden Staircase (#2)

The Bungalow Mystery (#3)

The Mystery of Lilac Inn (#4)

The Secret at Shadow Ranch (#5)

The Secret of Red Gate Farm (#6)

The Clue in the Diary (#7)

Nancy's Mysterious Letter (#8)

The Sign of the Twisted Candles (#9)

Password to Larkspur Lane (#10)

The Clue of the Broken Locket (#11)

The Message in the Hollow Oak (#12)

The Mystery of the Ivory Charm (#13)

The Whispering Statue (#14)

The Haunted Bridge (#15)

The Clue of the Tapping Heels (#16)

Mystery of the Brass-Bound Trunk (#17)

The Mystery at the Moss-Covered Mansion (#1

The Quest of the Missing Map (#19)

The Clue in the Jewel Box (#20)

The Secret in the Old Attic (#21)

The Clue in the Crumbling Wall (#22)

The Mystery of the Tolling Bell (#23)

The Clue in the Old Album (#24)

The Ghost of Blackwood Hall (#25)

The Clue of the Leaning Chimney (#26)

The Secret of the Wooden Lady (#27)

The Clue of the Black Keys (#28)

Mystery at the Ski Jump (#29)

The Clue of the Velvet Mask (#30)

The Ringmaster's Secret (#31)

The Scarlet Slipper Mystery (#32)

The Witch Tree Symbol (#33)

The Hidden Window Mystery (#34)

The Haunted Showboat (#35)

The Secret of the Golden Pavillion (#36)

The Clue in the Old Stagecoach (#37)

The Mystery of the Fire Dragon (#38)

The Clue of the Dancing Puppet (#39)

The Moonstone Castle Mystery (#40)

Clue of the Whistling Bagpipes (#41)

The Phantom of Pine Hill (#42)

The Mystery of the 99 Steps (#43)

The Clue in the Crossword Cipher (#44)

The Spider Sapphire Mystery (#45)

The Invisible Intruder (#46)

The Mysterious Mannequin (#47)

The Crooked Banister (#48)

The Secret of Mirror Bay (#49)

The Double Jinx Mystery (#50)

Mystery of the Glowing Eye (#51)

The Secret of the Forgotten City (#52)

The Sky Phantom (#53)

The Strange Message in the Parchment (#54)

Mystery of Crocodile Island (#55)

The Thirteenth Pearl (#56)

This book has been bound
using handcraft methods and
Smyth-sewn to ensure durability.

The dust jacket and
interior were designed by
Ellen Lohse.

The text was written by
Jennifer Worick.

The text was edited by
Melissa Wagner.

The text was set in Lydian,
Goudy, and Cheltenham.